This book belongs to:

....

....

The Big ARTHUR Storybook

The Big ARTHUR Storybook

MARC BROWN

RED FOX

A Red Fox Book

Published by Random House Children's Books
20 Vauxhall Bridge Road, London SW1V 2SA

A division of Random House UK Ltd
London Melbourne Sydney Auckland
Johannesburg and agencies throughout the world

1 3 5 7 9 10 8 6 4 2

This edition first published in Great Britain by Red Fox 1999

All books first published in the United States of America
by Little, Brown and Company and simultaneously in
Canada by Little, Brown and Company (Canada) Ltd.
First published in Great Britain by Red Fox

Printed in Hong Kong.

RANDOM HOUSE UK Limited Reg. No. 954009

ISBN 0 09 940340 4

Arthur Adventures in this Book:

MARC BROWN

ARTHUR'S TEACHER TROUBLE

For Tucker Eliot Brown
A winner in my book every day!

The bell rang.

The first day of school was over.

Kids ran out of every classroom – every one but Room 13.

Here, the students filed out slowly, in alphabetical order.

"See you tomorrow," said their teacher, Mr Ratburn.

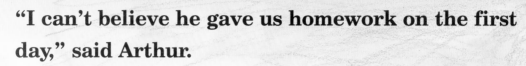

"I can't believe he gave us homework on the first day," said Arthur.

"I had the Rat last year," said Prunella. "Boy, do I feel sorry for you!"

"Make one wrong move," warned Binky Barnes, "and he'll really make you pay for it."

"He's really a vampire with magical powers," said Chris.

As everyone was leaving, the head teacher came out of his office. "Are you ready for the September spellathon?" he asked.

"Yes!" cheered the crowd.

"Who's going to win this year?" asked the head.

"Me!" everyone shouted.

"If I win again this year, do I get my name on the trophy twice?" asked Prunella.

"Not if I can help it," whispered Francine.

When Arthur got home, he slammed the back door.
"How was school?" Mother asked.
"I got the strictest teacher in the whole world,"
grumbled Arthur.

"Have a chocolate chip cookie," said Mother.
"Don't have time," said Arthur. "I have tons of homework."
"I'll eat Arthur's," said D.W. "I don't have any homework."
"You don't even go to school," said Arthur.
"I know." D.W. smiled.

After dinner Arthur was still doing homework.
"What's that?" asked D.W.
"It's a map of Africa," said Arthur.
"Looks like a pepperoni pizza," said D.W. "Next
year when I'm in kindergarten, I won't have *any*
homework. Ms Meeker never gives it."
"Mom!" called Arthur. "D.W.'s being a pest."
"Time for bed," said Mother. "You can finish
your map of Florida in the morning."
"*Africa*," said Arthur.

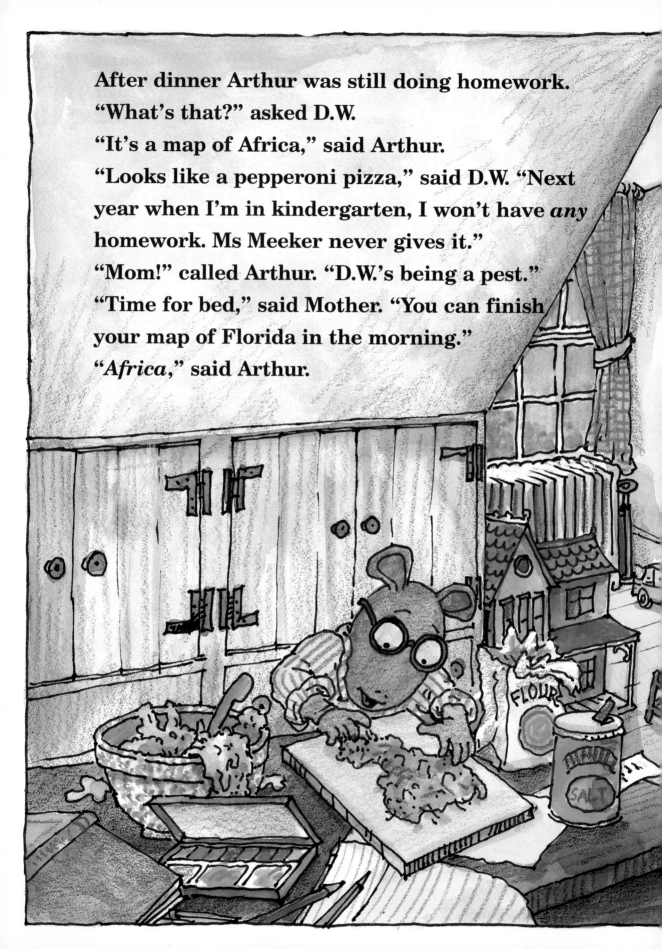

The next day, Mr Ratburn announced a spelling test for Friday. "I want you to study very hard," he said. "The test will have a hundred words." Buster looked pale.

"And," continued Mr Ratburn, "the two students with the highest scores will represent our class at the all-school spellathon."

That week everyone in Arthur's class studied harder than ever. Arthur spent a lot of time looking for quiet places to study.

Suddenly it was Friday and time for the test. Arthur could smell Miss Sweetwater's class making popcorn.

He could hear Mrs Fink's class leaving for a trip to the aquarium. "Why did *we* have to get stuck with the Rat?" he whispered to Francine.

Mr Ratburn marked their papers during lunch. "Class," he said, "most of you did very well in the test. But only two of you spelt *every* word correctly."

Muffy smiled. Francine hiccupped.

Buster patted his good-luck charm.

Mr Ratburn cleared his throat.

"Our class representatives for the spellathon will
be the Brain and Arthur."
"There must be some mistake!" said Muffy.

Mr Ratburn gave Arthur and the Brain each a special list of words. "Just study these and you'll be ready for the spellathon in two weeks," he said.

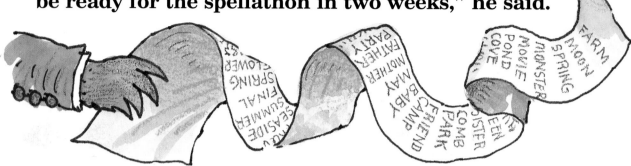

Arthur's family helped him study.
Grandma asked Arthur
his spelling words.

"How about your C-H-O-R-E-S?" Father asked.
"Have you made your B-E-D?" Mother added.

D.W. helped, too.
When Francine and Buster came over,
D.W. answered the door.
"Arthur can't play, but I can," she said. "I don't have to study."

"I can't believe the spellathon is finally here," said Grandma.

"Maybe now we'll get a little peace and quiet," D.W. said.

"Good luck, Arthur," said Mother and Father.

From backstage Arthur could hear the whole
school out in the auditorium.

"Well, today's the big day," said Mr Ratburn.

"How do you feel?"

"I feel fine," the Brain answered.

Arthur gulped. "I wish I were still back in bed!"

The head welcomed everyone and explained
the rules.

The Brain had the first turn. He stepped up to the
microphone.

"The first word is *fear*," said the head.

"F-E-R-E," said the Brain, a little too quickly.

"I'm sorry," said the head. "That's not correct."

"Are you sure?" asked the Brain.

"What dictionary are you using?"

The Brain wasn't the only one to drop out quickly.
The representatives from Miss Sweetwater's and
Mrs Fink's class were gone in a flash.
Before long, only Arthur and Prunella were left.

It was Prunella's turn.

"The word is *preparation*," said the head.

Prunella looked down at her feet.

"Could I have the definition, please?" she asked after a moment.

"Preparation," the head repeated. "The process of getting ready."

"Of course," said Prunella. "P-R-E-P," she paused,

"E-R-A-T-I-O-N."

"I'm sorry, that's incorrect," said the head.

"Now Arthur get's a chance to spell it."

Arthur looked out over the audience and took a deep breath.

"Preparation," he said. "P-R-E-P-A-R-A-T-I-O-N."

"Correct!" said the head.

Everyone in Mr Ratburn's class cheered.

Then Mr Ratburn went to the microphone. "I'm very proud of Arthur," he said. "In fact, I'm proud of my whole class. They worked very hard. This is the last third grade I'll have in the spellathon. But next year I look forward to a new challenge . . .

◇ FOR TOLON, TUCKER AND ELIZA ◇
my three babies

"We have a surprise for you," said Mother
and Father.
"Is it a bicycle?" asked Arthur.

"We're going to have a baby!" said Mother.
"Ooooo," squealed D.W. "I love babies!"
"A *baby*?" said Arthur.
"Yes, in about six months," said Father.
"Plenty of time for us all to get ready."

Arthur's friends had lots of advice.
"Better get some earplugs," said Binky Barnes,
"or you'll never sleep."

"Forget about playing after school," said Buster.
"You'll have to baby-sit."

"You'll have to change all those dirty nappies!" said Muffy.

"And you'll probably start talking baby talk," said Francine. "Doo doo ga ga boo boo."

For the next few months, everywhere
Arthur looked there were babies – more
and more babies.
"I think babies are taking over the world!"
said Arthur.

"Don't look now," said Buster,
"but you could be in for triple trouble."

One day after school, D.W. grabbed
Arthur's arm.
"I will teach you how to put a baby's nappy on," she said.
"Don't worry about nappies," said Mother.
"Come sit next to me. I want to show you
something."

Arthur age 9 months

"Is that really me?" asked Arthur.
"Yes," said Mother. "You were such a cute baby."

Arthur age 1 year

D.W. age 2 months

"Look," said D.W. "This is me with Mommy and Daddy. Don't I look adorable?"

D.W. age 5 months

That Saturday morning, Mother took out her suitcase.

"Where are you going?" asked Arthur.

"The baby could come any day now," said Mother.

"I need to be ready for the hospital."

"Here," said D.W. "Something for you to look at while you're there."

On Sunday morning, Arthur and D.W. found Grandma Thora making breakfast.

"You have a new sister!" she said.

"Yippee! Yippee! Yippee!" said D.W. "She'll be just like me!"

"That's what I'm afraid of," said Arthur.

The next day, they went to the hospital to see
the new baby.
"We named her Kate," said Father.
"I think she has your nose, Arthur."
"I think she has D.W.'s mouth," said Arthur.

On Tuesday, Mother and Father brought Kate home.
Everyone was acting like they'd never seen
a baby before.
Every time the doorbell rang, more presents arrived.
"They're not for you, Arthur," said D.W.
"They're for the baby."

"Arthur, don't you want to try holding Kate?"
Mother asked.
"Can I have another turn first?" asked D.W.
"It's Arthur's turn," Mother said.
"I'd rather look," said Arthur.
"It's just as well," said D.W.
"Arthur doesn't know beans
about babies."

A few days later, Mother needed some help.
"I have to go upstairs," she said. "Arthur, would
you watch Kate?"
"*Me?*" asked Arthur. "What do I do?"
"Don't worry," said D.W. "I'll take care
of everything."

When the doorbell rang, D.W. answered the door. "Arthur can't play," she said. "He has to baby-sit. But you can come in and see my baby."

"Don't get too close, because you all have germs!
And be quiet," D.W. said, "my baby is sleeping."

"Look!" said Francine. "She's opened her eyes."
"Stand back," said D.W. "She wants her bottle."

Kate drank her bottle in a flash.

Then she began to cry.
"Everyone remain calm," said D.W.

D.W. gave Kate a kiss.
Kate cried louder.

D.W. bounced Kate.
Kate screamed.

"Arthur, quick! Do something!" D.W. said.

"She's your baby, too."

"All of a sudden she's *my* baby," said Arthur.

"Why is she crying?" asked D.W.

"She's trying to tell you something," said Arthur.

"What?" asked D.W.

"Listen carefully," said Arthur.

"Burp!" said Kate.
"Is everything all right?" asked Mother.
"It is now," Arthur answered.

MARC BROWN

ARTHUR'S BIRTHDAY

FOR: Arthur
FROM: Francine

"I can't wait! I can't wait!" said Arthur.
"Are you sure it's only Tuesday?"
"See for yourself," said Mother.

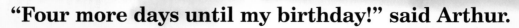

"Four more days until my birthday!" said Arthur.
"I hope everyone can come to my birthday party."
"What kind of cake should I bake?" asked
Grandma Thora.

"Chocolate!" said Arthur.

"Have a good day at school," said Mother, smiling.

"And don't forget to hand out your invitations," said D.W.

"Buster, can you come to my party?" asked Arthur.
"Are you kidding?" said Buster. "Of course!"
"Grandma's making chocolate cake," said Arthur.
"I'll be there!" said the Brain. "I love chocolate."

"How about me?" asked Binky Barnes.
"You're invited," said Arthur, "and Francine, too."
"Oh, boy," said Francine, "we can play spin
the bottle!"

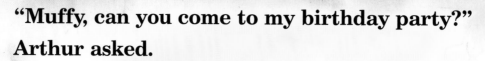

"Muffy, can you come to my birthday party?"
Arthur asked.

"Sure," Muffy answered. "When is it?"

"Saturday afternoon," Arthur said. "I can't wait."

"*This* Saturday afternoon? But that's when I'm having my party!" said Muffy.

"Oh, no!" said Arthur. "You can't. Can't you change your party to another day?"

"Are you kidding?" said Muffy. "The rock band and Pickles the Clown have been booked for months."

"I can't change my party, either," said Arthur. "All my relatives are coming from Ohio."

No one knew what to do.
Should they go to Arthur's
birthday party?

Or Muffy's?

On Wednesday before school, the boys had a meeting.

"I think we should stick together," said Buster.

"Me, too!" said Binky.

"Right!" said the Brain. "We're all going to Arthur's party."

"But what about the girls?" asked Arthur.

"Who needs girls?" said Buster.

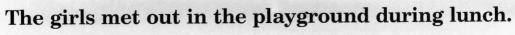

The girls met out in the playground during lunch.
"Anyone who doesn't come to my party can't be my
friend," said Muffy.
"But it won't be as much fun without the boys,"
said Francine.
"Are you my friend or not?" asked Muffy.

On Thursday after school, Arthur and his mother
picked out decorations for the party.
Later, the postman brought a big box.
"Wow! This weighs a ton!" said D.W.

In the post there were three birthday cards
for Arthur.
One was from Uncle Bud. When Arthur opened it,
three dollar bills fell out.
"Some people have all the luck!" said D.W.

On the way home from school on Friday, Arthur ran to catch up with Francine.

"I wish you could come to my party," said Arthur.

"I promised Muffy," said Francine. "But I wish I could go to both. What's a party without boys?"

"Wait a minute!" said Arthur.
"I have an idea."

"That's great," said Francine. "I'll help."

They ran to Arthur's tree house.
Arthur found pencils, paper and envelopes.
"Let me write them," said Francine. "It has to look
like Muffy's handwriting."
"OK," said Arthur, "but be sure there's one for
all the girls."

That night Arthur told his parents about his plan.
Early the next morning, Arthur and Francine
delivered their notes: one to Prunella, one to
Sue Ellen, and one to Fern.

The last note they delivered was a special one.
"All done," said Arthur.
"See you later!" said Francine.

"I can smell pancakes!" said Arthur when he got home.
"Your favourite," said Father.
"And maple syrup all the way from Ohio," said
Aunt Bonnie.
"Happy birthday!" said Cousin George.

"Time for birthday kisses," said Mother.
"And eight birthday hugs," said Grandma Thora.
"Don't forget a pinch to grow an inch!" said D.W.

PIN THE TAIL

Arthur stood by the window. It was almost noon.
"Someone's coming!" he cried.
It was Sue Ellen.

"What are you doing here?" asked Sue Ellen.
"What are you doing here?" asked Buster.
"It's a surprise for Muffy," said Francine, coming up behind them.
"It's a surprise for all of us!" said the Brain.
"Everyone find a place to hide," said Arthur.
"Muffy will be here any minute!"

"Shhhh!" whispered Buster. "Here she comes!"
Arthur opened the door.
"Hi, Arthur, I came to pick up my present,"
said Muffy.

"Surprise!" shouted everyone.
"Happy birthday, Muffy!" said Arthur.
"See I told you, your present is too big to carry."
"The rest of your party is on the way,"
said Francine.
"After all," said Arthur, "what's a birthday party
without all your friends!"

"This is the best birthday ever," said Muffy. "We should do this every year!"

"But next year at your house," said Arthur's mother.

"Time to open presents," said Francine. "I picked this one out especially for you. You have to promise me you'll use it right away."
"Sure," said Arthur. "I can't wait."

MARC BROWN

ARTHUR BABY-SITS

With love and thanks to some great readers and writers:
Barbara Bush; Ms. Cassell's class in Terre Haute, Indiana;
and Mary Etta Bitter's class in Lakewood, Ohio

Arthur's sister D.W. had a problem.

"The Tibble twins are visiting again, and they're driving
me crazy!" she said. "They're everywhere I go."

"Oh, they can't be that bad," said Arthur.

"How would you know?" said D.W.

Later that afternoon, Arthur and D.W. took Kate for a walk.

"Look!" shouted the Tibble twins. "There's D.W.!"

"Oh, no!" said D.W. "Quick, let's hide."

Mrs Tibble looked worried.

"I'm in a terrible pickle," she said. "I need a baby-sitter for my grandsons tonight, and I can't find one anywhere."

"Arthur will do it!" said D.W. "He baby-sits me all the time."

"Oh, Arthur, you're a life-saver!" said Mrs Tibble. "I'll call your mother and arrange it right now."

"Baby-sitting is such a big responsibility," said Arthur.
"I'm a little bit nervous."
"You'll do a good job," said Mother.
"We'll be right here if you want to call us," said Father.
"Here's my crash helmet," said D.W. "You'll need it!"
"Why?" asked Arthur. "Are you coming along?"
"You think *I'm* trouble?" said D.W. "Just wait."

On the way, Arthur walked past the Sugar Bowl.

"Hey, Arthur," called Buster, "where are you going?"

"I'm on my way to baby-sit for Mrs Tibble," said Arthur.

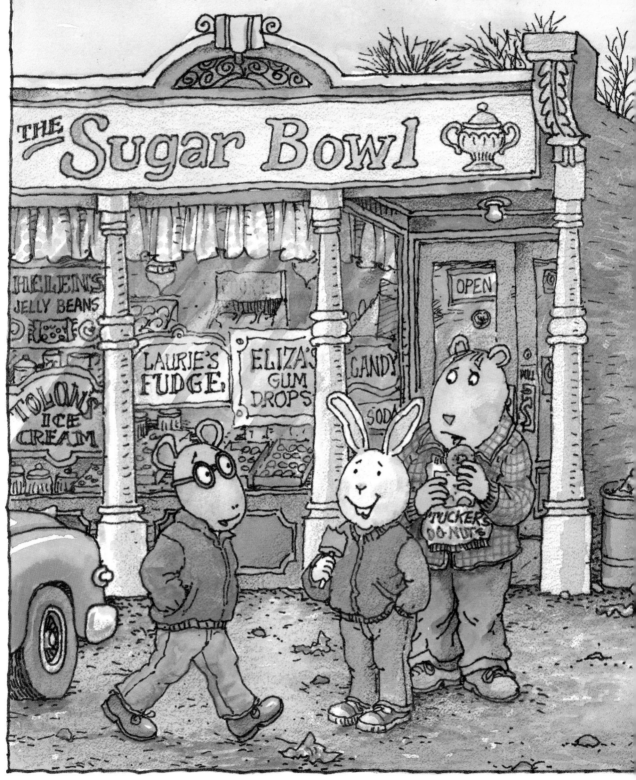

"Not the terrible Tibble twins!" gasped Prunella. "My sister baby-sat for them once. And *once* was enough."

"You can always back out," said Buster, ". . . while you're still alive."

"Don't worry," said Francine. "It will be just like baby-sitting D.W. and Baby Kate."

Arthur remembered what that was like!

Now he was really worried.

Mrs Tibble was waiting for Arthur.

"I'm so glad you're here," she said. "And so are the twins. This is little Tommy in red, and Timmy's in blue. Almost bedtime, darlings! I'll be back soon."

"Very soon, I hope," said Arthur.

"Nighty-night, Grammy," said the twins sweetly.

"She's gone!" screamed the twins. "Playtime!"

BANG!

BANG!

BANG!

"No, *bed*time," said Arthur.

"We're not sleepy," said Timmy.

The phone rang. It was D.W.

"I'm calling with some advice," she said. "Calm them down with a quiet game . . . like cards."

"Thanks," said Arthur. "Bye."

"How about a nice quiet game of cards?" asked Arthur.

"Great!" said the twins.

"We know a really good card game . . ." said Tommy.

"Fifty-two card pick-up!" they screamed.
Just then the phone rang again. It was D.W.
"It sounds like they're out of control," she said. "You need
to show them who's boss!"
"Thanks a lot," said Arthur.

"Let's play cowboys!" said Tommy.

"I'll be the sheriff," said Arthur, "because I'm the boss."

"And we'll be the bad guys," said Timmy.

The next time the phone rang, Timmy answered it.
"Arthur can't come to the phone right now," he said.
"He's all tied up."
"Time for hide-and-seek!" called Tommy. "You'll never
find us!"

When Arthur finally got loose, he searched and searched.
"If I don't find them soon," he thought, "I'll be in big trouble."

Just then the phone rang again.

"What's going on over there?" asked D.W. "Shouldn't they be in bed?"

"I can't talk now," said Arthur. "I'm looking for the twins."

"You mean you've lost them?" shouted D.W.

"Not exactly," he said. "I just can't find them."

"You're in really big trouble!" said D.W. "What are you going to do?"

Just then Arthur noticed the curtains wiggling.
"You'll see," he said. "I just hope I find them before the
swamp thing does!" he added loudly.
"Swamp thing?" asked Tommy from behind the curtain.

"Yes, the one that comes out on nights just like tonight,"
Arthur said. "Sit down and I'll tell you all about it."
Arthur used his spookiest voice. "Once upon a time in a dark,
spooky swamp, there lived a horrible, big, slimy, stinky green
swamp thing," he began.
"You mean like a monster?" Tommy asked meekly.
"Exactly," said Arthur, "with long, sharp teeth. And the
swamp thing realized it was very, very hungry," said Arthur.
"It left the swamp in search of dinner."
"What did it like to eat?" Timmy asked in a shaky voice.
"Boys," said Arthur. "Especially twin boys."

The twins moved closer to Arthur.

"The swamp thing began to moan from hunger," continued Arthur, "until it came to a big old house, just like this one."

"I can hear footsteps!" cried Timmy.

"It's only your imagination," said Arthur. "Do you want to sit on my lap?"

"Well, just for a minute," said Timmy.

"Slowly . . ." whispered Arthur, "with its big slimy green hand, the swamp thing opened the front door . . . 'I smell dinner,' it said. It licked its lips."

"Help!" screamed the twins.

"It's coming in *our* front door!" yelled Timmy.

Just then the door *did* open, and the lights came on.

"I'm home!" said Mrs Tibble. "And look at my little angels. Arthur must be a wonderful baby-sitter."

"He's not scared of anything," said Timmy.

"And he tells great stories, too!" said Tommy. "We want him to baby-sit us again."

The twins hugged Arthur good night.

Then Mrs Tibble paid Arthur and thanked him for doing such a good job.

When Arthur got home, D.W. was still up.

"You're home early," she said. "Have you been fired?"

"No," said Arthur. "Baby-sitting isn't so bad. Mrs Tibble thinks I'm pretty good at it. Now she wants me to baby-sit the twins every afternoon right here at our house. And . . .

"... since you know so much about baby-sitting, *you* can help!"

ARTHUR'S
PET BUSINESS

For Stan and Bill Eloranta,
who helped make my new treehouse studio happen.
M.B.

"You've been looking at puppies for months,"
said D.W.
"When are you going to ask Mom and Dad
if you can have one?"
"I'm waiting for the right moment,"
said Arthur, "so promise not to say anything!"

That night at dinner, Father asked,
"What's new?"
"Arthur wants a puppy," said D.W.
"Blabbermouth!" said Arthur.

"A puppy is a big responsibility," said Father.
"I can take care of it," said Arthur.
"We'll think about it," Mother said.
"That means no," explained D.W.

After dinner Mother and Father did the dishes.
"Can you hear what they're saying?" asked Arthur.
"They're worried about the new carpet," whispered D.W.
Suddenly the door opened.

"We've decided you may have a puppy if you can take care of it," said Father.

"Wow!" said Arthur.

"But," said Mother, "first you need to show us you're responsible."

"How will I ever prove I'm responsible?" asked Arthur.
"The best way I know is to get a job," said D.W.
"Then you can pay back the seven dollars you owe me!"
"Ka-chingg!" went her cash register.

Arthur wondered what kind of
job he could do.
"You could work for my dad
at the bank," said Muffy.
"He needs some new cashiers."

"If I were you, I'd get a job
at Joe's Junk Yard crushing
old cars," offered Binky Barnes.

"Do something that *you* like,"
said Francine.
That gave Arthur an idea.

"I'll take care of other people's pets," said Arthur,
"then Mom and Dad will know I can take care
of my own."

Arthur and Francine put up signs to advertise
his new business.

His family helped, too.

Arthur waited and waited. Then, just before bedtime, the phone rang.

"Hello," he said, "Arthur's Pet Business. How may I help you?

"Yes. No. When? Where? Great!" said Arthur.

"Hooray! I'm going to take care of Mrs Wood's dog
while she's on holiday, and I'll earn ten dollars!"
"Oh, no!" said D.W. "Not nasty little Perky?"
"Isn't that the dog the postman calls 'JAWS'?"
asked Father.
"That's Perky!" said D.W.

The next morning, Arthur ran all the way to
Mrs Wood's house.
"Right on time!" said Mrs Wood.
"*Grrrrr*," growled Perky.

"She hasn't been herself lately," said Mrs Wood. "I'm worried."

"I'll take good care of her," said Arthur. "We'll be best friends."

"*Grrrrr*," growled Perky.

"Here's her schedule and a list of things she doesn't like," said Mrs Wood. "I'll see you next Sunday."

Arthur did his best to make
Perky feel at home.
Every day he brushed her.
He tried to make her
favourite food.
They took lots of long walks –
day and night.
Perky made sure they had the whole
pavement to themselves.

"You look exhausted," said Mother. "Maybe taking care of a dog is too much work . . ."
"Any dog I get will be easier than Perky," said Arthur.

Word of Arthur's pet business got around.
On Monday the MacMillans asked Arthur to watch
their canary, Sunny.

On Tuesday Prunella gave Arthur
her ant farm.

On Wednesday the Brain asked
Arthur to take care of his frogs
while he went on holiday.

Best of all, on Thursday The Amazing Larry
asked Arthur to keep Cuddles,
his trained boa constrictor.

Animals were everywhere
– until Mother put her foot down.
"I want all these animals in the basement *now*!"
she ordered.

By bedtime all the pets were downstairs.
All except Perky.
Perky slept in Arthur's room.

On Saturday Buster asked Arthur to go to the movies.
"I can't," said Arthur. "When I finish cleaning these
cages, it will be feeding time.
"And anyway, it's Perky's last night with me and she
looks ill. I don't want to leave her."

"Well, I bet you're happy today," said D.W.
the next morning.
"You get rid of Perky and collect ten dollars!"
"I can't believe it," said Arthur.
"But I'm going to miss Perky."

"Arthur, Mrs Wood just called to say she's
on her way over," said Mother.
"Now, wait here, Perky," ordered Arthur.
"I'll go and get your lead."

When Arthur went back into the kitchen,
Perky was gone.

"Here Perky! Perky!" called Arthur.

But Perky didn't come.

"She's not in the basement," called Father.

"She's not in the garden," said D.W.

"She's lost!" said Arthur.

"Oh, oh!" said D.W. "You're in big trouble!"

"Arthur, Mrs Wood is here!" called Mother.

"Hi, Mrs Wood," said D.W. "Guess what?
Arthur lost Perky!"

"My poor little darling is lost?" asked Mrs Wood.

"Don't worry," said Father. "Arthur's looking for
her right now."

Suddenly they heard a bark.

"Everybody come quick!" called Arthur.

"Look," said Arthur. "Perky's had puppies!"
"No wonder she's been acting so strangely,"
said Mrs Wood.
"You've done a wonderful job taking care of Perky,
when she needed a friend the most.
How can I ever thank you?"

"A reward might be nice," suggested D.W.

"Shush!" said Mother.

"Here's the money I owe you," said Mrs Wood.

"And, how would you like to keep one of Perky's puppies as a special thank you?"

"I'd love to," said Arthur. "If I'm allowed."

"Of course," said Mother. "You've earned it."

"Wow!" said Arthur.
"Ten dollars *and* my very own puppy!
I can't believe it!"
"Neither can I," said D.W. "Now you can finally pay
back my seven dollars."
"Ka-chingg!" went her cash register.

MARC BROWN

ARTHUR'S NEW PUPPY

With thanks to Dorothy Crawford, the Kriegstein family,
and the lucky dogs in their lives.

Arthur loved his new puppy.
And Pal loved Arthur.
"He's a very active puppy," said Arthur.
"He's a very *naughty* puppy," said D.W.
"Don't worry," said Arthur. "I'll have him trained in no time."

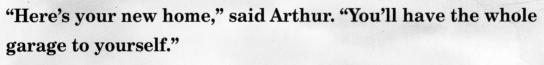

"Here's your new home," said Arthur. "You'll have the whole garage to yourself."

But Pal did not like the garage.

As soon as Arthur put him down, Pal ran and hid.

"He feels lonely," said Arthur. "Can he stay indoors? Please, please, please?"

"Oh, all right," said Mother, "but only for a day or two."

Arthur made a cosy spot for Pal in the kitchen.
"I thought you might need a few newspapers," said D.W.
Arthur held Pal carefully, just the way it said to in his
puppy book.
"Look, he's so excited," said Arthur.

"Look at your trousers," said D.W. "You have excitement all over them."

"It's OK," said Arthur. "He's just a baby."

"Well, I think baby dogs should wear nappies," said D.W.

Later on, Pal ate his dinner in a flash.

"Oh, oh," said D.W. "He has that look in his eyes again."

"Quick," said Arthur. "His lead."

But when Pal saw his lead, he ran and hid.

"I don't think he likes his lead," said D.W.

"Help me find him," said Arthur.

"I guess he didn't have to go after all," said D.W. "I was wrong."

"No, you were right," said Arthur. "He's just been."

Later that night, when everyone was asleep, Pal yelped and howled until he woke up the entire family.

"Go to sleep," said Arthur.

Pal wanted to play.

"Don't forget to close his gate," called Mother.

"Good night," said Father.

"Good luck," said D.W.

The next morning Arthur was still in the kitchen.
"Wake up, sleepy-head," said D.W., "and be careful
where you tread."
"Oh, no," said Arthur, "I forgot to close Pal's gate."
"Here's your scooper," said Mother.
"If you think this is bad," said Father, "wait until you
see the living room."

Pal looked very proud of himself.
"My new curtains," cried Mother.
"My doll!" screamed D.W.
"Bad dog!" said Arthur.

"Pal is moving into the garage," ordered Mother.

"Here's the key to the garage," said Father.

"I'll help you move his things after dinner."

Father put the key on the hall table.

Arthur packed up Pal's things and went to get the garage
key, but it had gone.
The whole family searched for the key.
Pal watched.
"It has to be here somewhere," said Mother.
But the key was nowhere to be found.

"It looks like you can stay in the house one more night," Arthur said.

"I heard Mom and Dad whispering," said D.W., "and Pal's in big trouble. They said he'd better be trained soon or else!"

"Shushh!" said Arthur. "You'll hurt his feelings."

That night, Arthur remembered to close Pal's gate.

At school, Arthur told Francine and Buster all about training Pal. "I'm going to teach him to do all kinds of things!" said Arthur.

"I used to have a puppy, too," said Buster.
"But he was too much trouble. My parents sent him to a farm."

"My cousin had a problem puppy," said Francine, "No one could train him. One day he just disappeared while she was at school."
After school Arthur hurried home.

"Oh, no!" said Arthur. "What happened?"
"I thought I'd take him for a walk," said D.W. "But when he saw the lead, he went wild! You'd better get this cleaned up before Mom sees it."

"Where is Mom?" asked Arthur.

"In the garden," said D.W. "Looking for the garage key."

"Have you seen my dog-training book?" asked Arthur.

"What's left of it is over there," said D.W.

That night Arthur gave Pal an extra training lesson.
"I'll help you train this monster," said D.W. "He needs
a good spank."
"No!" said Arthur. "Dogs respond better to love."
"Watch," said Arthur. "He's getting better."
"Sit," said Arthur.

"Lie down," said Arthur.

"Stay," ordered Arthur.

"I know something he'll understand," said D.W.
"Time for your walk, Pal."

"He just needs a little more work, that's all," said Arthur.

But Pal needed a lot more work.

Arthur set up a training school in the garden.

On Monday, they worked on "sit".

On Tuesday, they worked on "down".

Wednesday was "stay" day.

By Thursday, Pal was doing tricks.

"Good dog, Pal," said Arthur. Arthur decided to put on a puppy show for his family. "When they see how well you're trained, they'll never send you away," said Arthur.

Arthur got up early on Saturday morning to give Pal a bath.

After breakfast, Arthur's family took their seats.

"Welcome to Arthur's Puppy Show," said Arthur. He held his breath. "What you are about to see will amaze and astound you!"

"If Pal amazes us any more, our whole house will be destroyed," said D.W.

Arthur clapped his hands.
"Come!" he said.
And Pal came.

"Sit," said Arthur.
And Pal sat.

"Down," said Arthur.
Down went Pal.

Pal even did a trick.
"Good dog!" said Arthur.

"He *is* a good dog," said Mother.

"You mean he won't have to live on a farm?" asked Arthur.

"Of course not," said Father, "not even in the garage."

No one noticed Pal run behind the rose-bushes . . .

. . . when Pal came back, he sat up and wagged his tail.
"Look, he has something in his mouth," said D.W.
"It's the key to the garage!" said Arthur.
"Good boy, Pal," said Father.
"Amazing!" said Mother.

That night Arthur gave Pal a special dinner.

"Time for your walk, Pal!" said Arthur. "I'll get your lead."

But Arthur couldn't find it anywhere.

"It was on the hook a minute ago," said Arthur.

"I know I left it there."

"I'll help you look," said D.W.

Mother and Father helped, too.

"It has to be here somewhere . . ." said Arthur.

No one had noticed Pal run behind the rose-bushes.

MARC BROWN

ARTHUR'S CHICKEN POX

For all the chicken pox experts in Mrs Bundy's class at DeWitt Road School,
with love and thanks!

It was Monday morning, but Arthur's family were thinking about Saturday's trip to the circus.

"I wonder if the knife thrower will be back," said Father.

"The trapeze artists are my favourite," said Mother.

"I like the clowns best," said Arthur.

"I like the candyfloss," said D.W.

Arthur thought about the circus at school, too.

For his art project, he drew a picture of the circus.

Then at lunch time, Arthur noticed he didn't feel very well.

He went to see the school nurse.

"You've got a temperature," said the nurse.
Then Arthur's dad arrived to take him home.
"I'm going to get better fast," said Arthur. "I don't want to miss the circus."

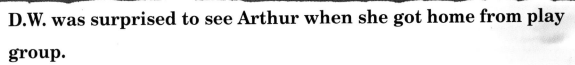

D.W. was surprised to see Arthur when she got home from play group.

"What's wrong with you?" she asked. "You don't look very ill to me."

"But I *feel* ill," said Arthur.

"I think you're faking," said D.W.

At dinner time, Arthur was allowed to have chicken noodle soup sitting on the sofa.

"Why do I have to eat at the table?" asked D.W.

"You're not ill," said Mother.

"Well, I think Arthur is just pretending," said D.W.

"Eat your spinach," said Father.

The next morning, Arthur was *really* ill.

"Arthur's all spotty!" said D.W., laughing. "It's too bad he'll miss the circus."

"I'll see if Grandma Thora can stop by later," said Mother. "She knows all about chicken pox."

That afternoon, Grandma Thora arrived.

"I've brought you some treats to help you feel better," she said.

After school, Arthur's friends stopped by with get well cards.

Muffy brought Arthur all his homework.

Father brought Arthur some stickers and cherry-flavoured cough drops.

"Can I have a cough drop too?" asked D.W.

"You're not ill," said Arthur.

"I feel all itchy," said Arthur after dinner.

"Try not to scratch," said Grandma Thora.

"But I want to scratch," said Arthur.

"I'll make a special soothing bath," said Grandma Thora.

"That might help."

Arthur was allowed to drink juice in the bathtub with a crazy
straw.
"If you're a good boy and don't scratch your spots," said D.W.,
"I'll bring you home a balloon from the circus."

After his bath, Grandma Thora gave Arthur a back rub and told him a story.

"I think I'm ready for my hot lemon drink now," said Arthur.
"And don't forget the extra honey! Please!"
"Can I have a back rub, too?" asked D.W.
"Maybe later," said Grandma Thora. "Right now I've got to get
Arthur's drink."
Suddenly, D.W. had an idea.

She went into the bathroom and closed the door.

First D.W. put baby powder on her face to look pale.

Then she looked through her box of pens for a pink one.

And she gave herself spots – lots of spots.

D.W. made loud moaning sounds as she came down the stairs.

"I don't feel well," she said.

"Good heavens," said Grandma Thora. "Now you've got spots, too! Let me take your temperature."

When no one was looking, D.W. held the thermometer under the hot water tap.

"Oh, dear," said Grandma Thora when she read the thermometer.

"I feel itchy, too," said D.W. "I think I need a soothing bath."

"Of course," said Grandma Thora.

"And how about some juice," asked D.W., "with a crazy straw?"

"Of course, darling," said Grandma Thora.

D.W. didn't notice that while she was in the bathtub, all her
pink spots had washed right off.
But Grandma Thora noticed.
"Dora Winifred!" she scolded. "I'm very disappointed in you."

"Well, how's our little patient?" D.W. asked Arthur the next afternoon.

"Still itchy," said Arthur. "And still ill."

"That's too bad" said D.W.

She moved the telephone nearer to Arthur.

"Excuse me," she said. "I have to make an important call."

"Hello, Emily? I've got an extra ticket for the circus on Saturday. Want to go with me? . . . Great! Bye."

"Mom!" moaned Arthur. "D.W. is torturing me."

By Friday, Arthur was feeling well enough to go out to dinner with his family.

"I think I'll be going to the circus after all," he said.

"Oh, that's just grand," said Grandma Thora.

"D.W., you'd better call Emily," said Mother.

"Maybe I should wait," said D.W. "Who knows? Arthur might get the flu."

But Arthur didn't get the flu.

The next morning, he was up early and dressed for the circus.

Everyone else was ready for the circus, too.

Everyone except D.W.

"Hurry up, D.W., or we'll be late," called Mother.

D.W. came down the stairs singing, "It's candyfloss I love to eat.

It's so squishy. It's so sweet."

Mother just looked at D.W.
"Oh, boy," said Father.

"Good heavens," said Grandma Thora.

Arthur started laughing.

"What's so funny?" asked D.W.

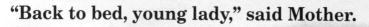

"Back to bed, young lady," said Mother.

"But what about the circus?" cried D.W.

"Don't worry," said Arthur. "If you're a good little girl and don't scratch, I'll bring you home a balloon."

MARC BROWN

ARTHUR'S TV TROUBLE

For my friend Paula Danziger

It all started while Arthur was watching *The Bionic Bunny Show*.

"Dogs love 'em," said the announcer. "The amazing Treat Timer. Treat your pet to a Treat Timer. Only $19.95. Treats may vary. Batteries not included. If you love your pet – get a Treat Timer!"

"Wow!" said Arthur. "Pal needs one of those."

Adverts for the Treat Timer were everywhere.

Now Arthur really wanted one.

Arthur counted his money. D.W. helped.

"Even with all my birthday money," he said, "I only have ten dollars and three cents."

"I know what you're thinking," said D.W.

She ran to protect her cash register.

Arthur decided to ask Father if he could have his pocket money early.

"Gee, I'd love to help," said Father, "but my catering business is a little slow right now."

Arthur knew Mother would understand.

On the way to school, Arthur was walking very slowly.
"What are you doing?" asked Buster.

"Looking for money," said Arthur. "I want to buy Pal a Treat Timer."

"Those are very expensive," said Buster. "You need a job."

"I need a miracle," said Arthur.

At school, while everyone else did a spelling test, Arthur daydreamed about the Treat Timer. Mr Ratburn asked Arthur to stay behind after school to do the test again.

Arthur took the long way home so he could think of a good excuse for why he was late. Mr Sipple was clearing out his garage.

"Hi, Arthur," he said. "Every fifty years I clean the place
up. I could do with a little help."
"I could do with a little money," said Arthur.

"All these newspapers need to be recycled," said Mr Sipple. "I'll pay you fifty cents a stack to take them out onto the curb."

"Great!" said Arthur. "I'll do it tomorrow."

"I won't be home until after dinner," said Mr Sipple, "but you can get started. Everything you need to do the job is here."

"I'm rich!" thought Arthur.
All of a sudden, Arthur was in a big hurry to get home.

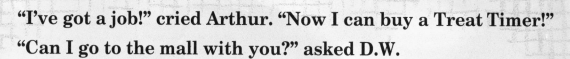

"I've got a job!" cried Arthur. "Now I can buy a Treat Timer!"

"Can I go to the mall with you?" asked D.W.

"Sure," said Arthur.

"I wish you were rich all the time," said D.W. "You're much nicer."

The next day, Arthur counted the stacks as he pulled them onto the curb. Twenty-four.

"That makes twelve whole dollars!" cried Arthur. "I'll come back later to collect my money!"

"You look exhausted," said D.W. when Arthur got home. "I don't want to see another newspaper for a long, long time," said Arthur.

"Well, then don't look out of the window," said D.W.

"So *that's* what the string was for!" said Arthur. "I'd better hurry before Mr Sipple gets home."

"Wait for me," said D.W.

"You're in big trouble," said D.W.

"You've missed some over there.

These stacks could be a lot neater.

Are you using double knots?"

"Nice work!" said Mr Sipple when he got home. "Here's your twelve dollars."

"Thank you," said Arthur.

"I helped too," said D.W. "Don't I get something?"

"You get a trip to the mall, remember?" said Arthur.

The next morning, Arthur and his family were the first
ones at the mall. Arthur put his money on the counter.
"One Treat Timer, please," he said.
"It looks bigger on TV," said Arthur when he saw the box.
"You have to assemble it, of course," said the salesperson.
"And remember, all sales are final."

Five hours later, the Treat Timer was ready.
"You're going to love it, Pal," said Arthur.
Pal sniffed it.
Arthur turned it on. It clicked. Lights flashed.

Treats shot out like rockets.
Pal let out a loud bark and ran for cover.
"Turn it off!" yelled Mother.

"I'm trying to," said Arthur. "But I think it's broken."
"And remember," said D.W., "all sales are final."
Arthur went up to his room to be alone.

"I'm worried," said Mother. "He's been up there for hours."
"I know how to get him down," said D.W.
"It's seven o'clock," she yelled up the stairs. "*The Bionic Bunny Show* is on!"

Seconds later, Arthur appeared.

"Sit down," said D.W., "so I can protect you from those nasty adverts."

"I don't need these!" said Arthur. "There's no way a TV ad will get all my hard-earned money again."

"It's the Magic Disappearing Box!" said the announcer.

"Astound your friends! Eliminate your enemies! The Magic Disappearing Box from KidTricks!"

"Hmmm," said Arthur. "Now, this could be useful."

"What would you ever do with that?" asked D.W.

MARC BROWN

ARTHUR
WRITES A STORY

for Phyllis Wender

Arthur's teacher, Mr Ratburn, was explaining their homework.
"What should the story be about?" Arthur asked.
"Anything," Mr Ratburn said. "Write about something that is important to you."

Arthur started his story the minute he got home.
He knew exactly what he wanted to write about.

How I Got My Puppy Pal

I always wanted a dog, but first I had to prove I was responsible. So I started Arthur's Pet Business. My mom made me keep all the animals in the basement. It was a lot of work, but it was fun until I thought I lost Perky. But then I found her, and she had three puppies! And I got to keep one of them. That's how I got my dog Pal.

The End

Arthur read his story to D.W.

"That's a boring story," D.W. said. "Does it have to be about real life? Because your life is so dull."

"I don't want to write a boring story," said Arthur.

"If it were me," D.W. suggested, "I'd make the story about getting an elephant."

The next day, Arthur read his new story to Buster.
"Did you like the part about the elephant puppies?"
he asked.
"It's OK, I guess," said Buster. "I'm writing a cool story
about outer space."

Maybe my story should take place on the moon, thought Arthur.

On Wednesday, Arthur read his latest story to the Brain. "Scientifically speaking, elephants would weigh less on the moon, but they wouldn't float that high," said the Brain.

"So you don't like it?" asked Arthur.

"A good story should be well researched," said the Brain.

"Like mine. It's called, 'If I Had a Pet Stegosaurus in the

Jurassic Period'."

Arthur hurried to the library.

"What are all those books for?" asked Francine.

"Research," said Arthur. "I'm writing about my pet
five-toed mammal of the genus *Loxodonta*."

"Your *what*?" asked Francine.

"My elephant!" Arthur explained.

"Oh," said Francine. "I'm putting jokes in my story."

All through dinner, Arthur worried about his story.
"Please pass the corn on the cob," said Father.

"Corn! That's it!" said Arthur. "Purple corn and blue elephants! On Planet Shmellafint! Now *that*'s funny."
"Arthur is acting weirder than usual," said D.W.

On Thursday, everyone at the Sugar Bowl was talking about their stories.

"Last year, a kid wrote a country-and-western song for her story," said Prunella. "And she got an A+."

"How do you know?" asked Arthur.

"That kid was me," explained Prunella. "Mr Ratburn said I should send it to a record company. It was *that* good."

"Wow!" said Arthur.

That night, Arthur's imagination went wild. He decided to turn his story into a song. He even made up a dance to go with it.

Later, he tried it out on his family.
". . . Now this little boy
Can go home and enjoy
His own personal striped elephant.
And you will see
How happy he will be
Here on Planet . . . Shmellafint!"

"Well," said Arthur. "What do you think?"

Mother and Father smiled.

"It's nice," said Grandma Thora. "But a little confusing."

"Too bad you can't dance," said D.W.

"What am I going to do?" said Arthur. "My story is
due in tomorrow."
That night Arthur didn't sleep very well.

The next day, Arthur worried until Mr Ratburn finally called him up to the front of the class.

When Arthur's song and dance was over, the classroom was
so quiet, it was almost spooky. Binky raised his hand.
"Did that really happen?"

Planet
Shmellafint

"Sort of," said Arthur. "It started as a story about how I got my dog."

"I'd like to hear that story," said Mr Ratburn.

"The title was 'How I Got My Puppy Pal'," said Arthur.
Arthur told how proud he was of his pet business and how
scared he was when Perky disappeared. And he told how
happy he was to find her under his bed and how surprised
he was to see her three puppies.

"And the best part is," said Arthur, "I got to keep one!"

Buster said, "I like that story better than your other one."

"Great story!" said Binky.

"I think Arthur's story was the best!" said Francine.

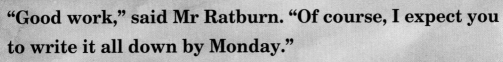

"Good work," said Mr Ratburn. "Of course, I expect you to write it all down by Monday."

Then Mr Ratburn gave Arthur a gold sticker. "Oh, and one more thing," he said.

MARC BROWN

ARTHUR'S COMPUTER DISASTER

For
Eliza Morgan Brown

"Mom, can I use your computer to play Deep, Dark Sea?"
asked Arthur.
"What's Deep, Dark Sea?" asked D.W.
"Only the greatest game in the universe," said Arthur.
"Can I, Mom, please?"

"What's the game about?" asked D.W.
"A haunted sunken ship," said Arthur.
"With skeletons, ghosts, and sharks."
"Sounds spooky," said D.W.

"Mom, please," begged Arthur.
"Oh, all right," said Mother, "but finish your dinner first."
Arthur finished his dinner in a jiffy.

Once Arthur started playing Deep, Dark Sea,
he couldn't stop.
"Time for bed," said Father.
"But Dad, I've almost found *the thing*," said Arthur.

"When I find *the thing*, I can win stuff."
"You can find *the thing* tomorrow," said Father.
"It's bedtime."
"I'm ready for bed," said D.W. sweetly.

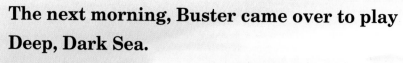

The next morning, Buster came over to play
Deep, Dark Sea.
"Sorry, boys," said Mother. "I'm really busy.
I need my computer all day."

Just then the phone rang. It was for Mother.
"I have to run to the office," she said. "Now don't touch
my computer."

After Mother had left, Arthur and Buster stared at
the computer.

"I know what you're thinking," said D.W.

"But I'm so close to finding *the thing*," said Arthur.

"You could probably find it before your mom gets home,"
said Buster.

"I'm telling Dad," warned D.W.

"I'll give you my desserts for a whole week," said Arthur.

"And play doll's house with me whenever I say so?"
asked D.W.

"Yes," grumbled Arthur.

"And call me Your Royal Highness . . . ?" asked D.W.

"Don't push it," said Arthur.

Arthur loaded up the game.
"Look out for the Squid Squad!" yelled Buster.
"I'm running out of oxygen," said Arthur.
"Look," said Buster. "A treasure chest!"

"That's it!" screamed Arthur. "That's *the thing*! I've found it!"

"Let me open it!" shouted Buster.

"I found it," argued Arthur.

They both dived for the mouse.

The keyboard crashed to the floor.
"Uh-oh," said Arthur.
"You're in big trouble," said D.W.

Just then the phone rang. Everyone jumped.

It was Mother.

"I won't be home until tonight," she said. "Everything
all right?"

"Umm, fine, just great," said Arthur.

"You know, Mom can tell when you're lying,"
whispered D.W.

"Maybe we can fix it before she gets home," said Arthur.

Arthur looked through the computer manual.
"There's nothing in here about Deep, Dark Sea accidents,"
he said.
"Are you sure you've got the right manual?" asked D.W.

"The Brain can fix anything," said Buster. "Let's ask him."
"Alan's not home," said the Brain's mother.

They checked the library.

They checked the museum.
Just when they were about to give up, they found him.

"Are you doing a science experiment?" asked Buster.
"No, I'm skipping stones," said the Brain. "It's fun!"

Everyone went back to Arthur's house.

The Brain examined the computer.

"Hmmm," said the Brain. He shook his head.

"That bad?" asked Arthur.

"It must be," said the Brain. "I can't find the problem."

"Well, thanks for trying," said Arthur.

"Now you're in really, really big trouble," said D.W.

"If the Brain can't fix it, who can?" said Buster.

"I have an idea," said Arthur.

Arthur explained his problem to the computer expert.
Then the computer expert explained how much it would
cost to repair.
"That's more birthday money than I'll ever see in my
whole life," said Arthur. "I'm doomed."

"We're all doomed," said D.W. "Because now Mommy will lose her job and we won't be able to keep our house and we'll all have to live in the cold on the street and we'll all get ammonia and probably die and it's all your fault, Arthur!"

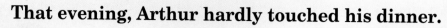

That evening, Arthur hardly touched his dinner.
"Hi, I'm home," called Mother.
"Mom, how about a game of cards?" asked Arthur.
"And a family bike ride?"

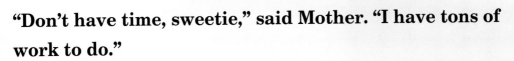

"Don't have time, sweetie," said Mother. "I have tons of
work to do."
Mother headed for the computer.
Arthur felt sick.

Arthur ran after Mother.
D.W. ran after Arthur.
Buster ran home.

Just as Mother's finger was about to hit the ON button,
Arthur yelled, "Stop!"
"I was playing Deep, Dark Sea, and the screen went blank.
I'm sorry. I've wrecked it. It's all my fault."

"That happens to me all the time," said Mother.
"Did you jiggle the switch?"
Mother jiggled the switch, and the game came on.
"Why didn't you call me?" asked Mother.
"Always call me with your problems."
"I thought you'd be cross," said Arthur.
"I'm not cross," said Mother. "I'm disappointed."

"Am I going to be punished?" asked Arthur.

"Of course," said Mother. "You did something you weren't supposed to do."

"Make the punishment really good," said D.W.

"No computer games for a week," said Mother. "Now, get ready for bed. I'll be up to say good night in a few minutes."

Arthur and D.W. did as they were told.
Then they waited for what seemed like a very long time.
"Mom," called Arthur. "Time to tuck us in."

"In a minute," said Mother. "The sharks are attacking!"
"Maybe we should tuck ourselves in tonight," said D.W.
"Good idea," said Arthur.

"I'll be right up," called Mother. "As soon as I blast these skeletons from the treasure chest."

"Good night, Mom," called D.W.
"Good night, Mom," called Arthur.